Ella: Who Am I?

La'Shaun Garcia

This book belongs to:

Ella: Who Am I?
A book about learning ones culture, race, and ethnicity in a fun way for all children and families. How to help answer the question of differences through example. Beautiful illustrations and simple text to show a child's curiosity and boldness through the love of family and togetherness.

v3.0 r1.1

Outskirts Press, Inc.
http://www.outskirtspress.com
https://outskirtspress.com/ellawhoami

ISBN: 978-1-4787-8755-6

Cover and interior images by Allison Gossett.

Outskirts Press and the "OP" logo are trademarks belonging to Outskirts Press, Inc.

PRINTED IN THE UNITED STATES OF AMERICA

Use Your QR App
To Learn More Today

This book is dedicated to the loves of my life, Urijah, Justin, Ella, and my family. To Rayona, who asked her TeTe this very important question. Allison, for bringing my story to life. I look forward to working with you in the future. To all the Ella's of the world, just know it's okay to LOOK and BE different.

Meet Ella. She is five years old. One day Ella asked her mommy an important question about her ethnicity. Your ethnicity means your physical characteristics, which is what you look like when you look in the mirror.

You see, Ella is both Mexican and African American.
Let's find out what Ella discovers...

As Ella sat in class nervously on the first day of school:

Her new kindergarten teacher came in front of the class and smiled.

She was the most beautiful teacher she had ever seen. She looked so different from everyone else, almost magical.

Being a curious little girl, Ella asked her teacher Mrs. Chang a question. "Mrs. Chang you're sooooo pretty, but why do you look so different from me?"

Ella looked around her class and noticed
she did not look like anyone else.

She began to get sad.

"Why thank you" Mrs. Chang replied, as she smiled so kindly. "My family is from China and I am Chinese American." "Ooooooh" Ella replied, "can I be Chinese too Mrs. Chang?"

"Oh Ella honey you come from a different ethnical background that is just as beautiful. Now when you get home, be sure to ask your mom and dad all about it. I know you will be very happy to learn more about your heritage."

"Otay!" Ella replied, and as soon as she got home she looked at her mommy and cried. "Oh mommy how come I don't look like You or Daddy? *Who Am I?*

I want to be Chinese like Mrs. Chang and I don't know my *ethny, ethicnee.*"

"Ethnicity" her mother said ever so gently.
"Yes!" Ella said. "And...and..."

Oh Ella cried and cried, and covered her face with her hands. Her mother could barely understand her words.

"Oh my dear Gabriella, why of course you look like mommy and daddy, I'll show you."

When Ella's mother returned she had a photo album titled, *Family Heritage*. Inside, Ella's mother showed her pictures of both sides of her family.

"You see, your father is Mexican American and can speak a different language. You know when Tia Camilla teaches you Spanish?" "Yes." Ella replied. "Spanish is apart of your heritage."

"Ella, you are also African American like mommy too."
"Do you know when we go to TeTe Shaunda's house, she is always teaching you how to cook different foods from Nana's recipe book?" "Yes!" Ella said, as she began to dry her eyes.

"That is also a part of your heritage and together, honey, it help shapes you. Our precious Gabriella Garcia. You see sweetheart, you look like both mommy and daddy."

Ella smiled the biggest smile ever and said to her mother, "Oh mommy, you mean I come from TWO ethnicities?" "Yes my dear, you do."

"Wow! Wait until I tell Mrs. Chang, she will be so happy." Ella hugged her mommy, and asked for her after school snack.

Later that night, Ella brushed her teeth with her parents. Ella's dad said, "look my sweet Ella, you have your mommy's beautiful eyes." Ella smiled.

"Oh honey, and you have your daddy's wonderful smile," said her mother.

At bedtime, Ella finished saying her prayers; she beamed with joy from her exciting day.

As mommy and daddy read a story and tucked her in, Ella smiled. She was proud of her heritage. After all, she may not look just like one of her parents, but she looked like both of them together, and she was very happy.

"Good night mommy and daddy." Ella whispered.
"Oh goodnight our dear Ella, we love you."

After the Story:

- Ask your child to look at the cover and identify a face that they may share a similar feature with & discuss what you find (Ex. Eye color, hair, glasses, or smile).
- Be a part of the story too! Have your child look in the mirror and draw a picture of themselves. (Have fun and draw each other or another family member as a child.) Add your photo to the classmates in Ella's head.
- Answer the question of differences that relate to your family in a fun positive way.

If you have any questions, please do not hesitate to contact La'Shaun.

Living in a world with many different cultures, it is important that we are all treated equally. We need to teach each other to be proud of who we are, no matter what we look like, or where we come from – that <u>all</u> are celebrated.

Visit her online at:

Ellawhoami@gmail.com
https://outskirtspress.com/ellawhoami

Milton Keynes UK
Ingram Content Group UK Ltd.
UKHW052228181223
434600UK00004B/41